W9-CJQ-709

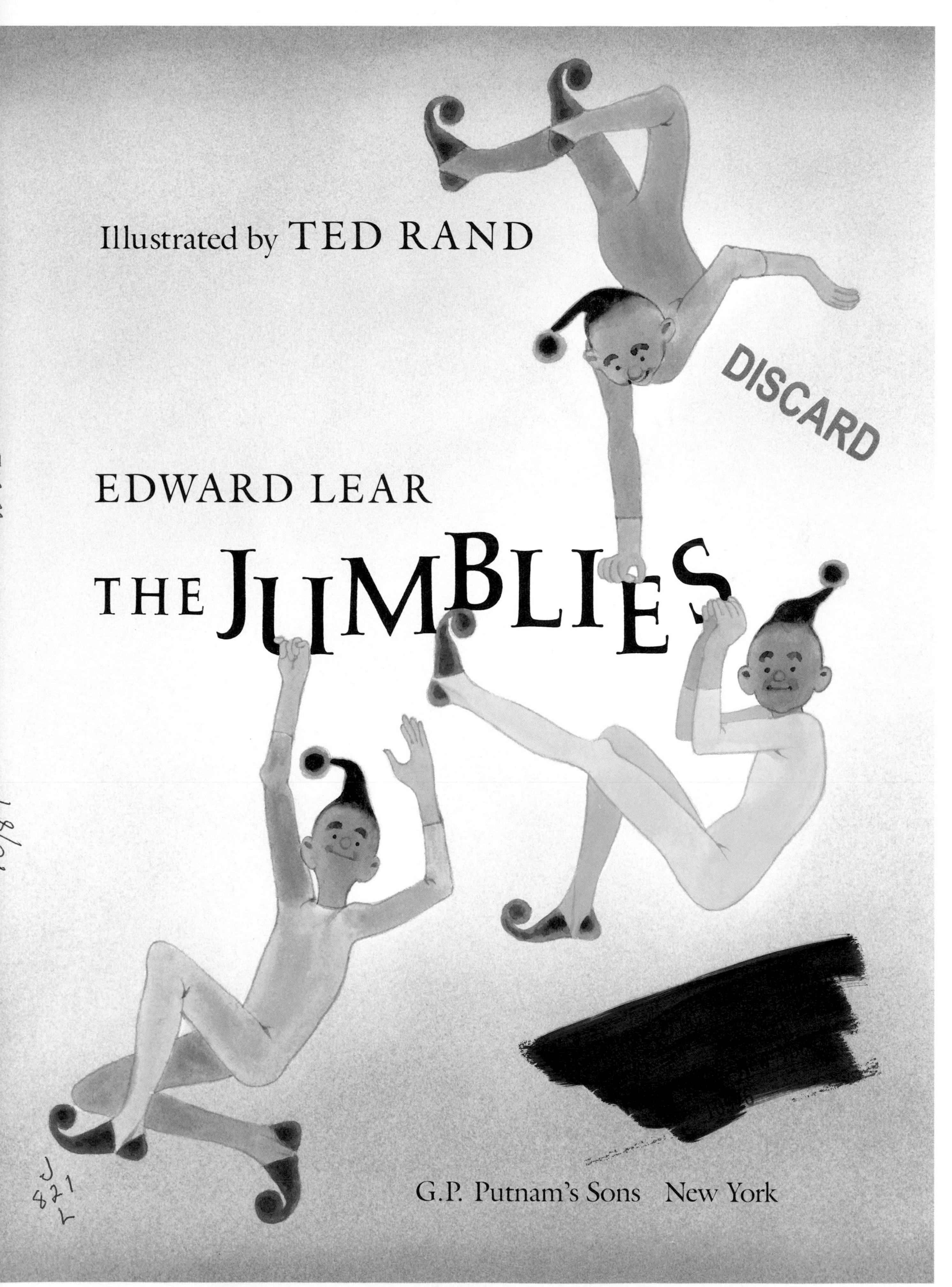

Illustrated by TED RAND

EDWARD LEAR

THE JUMBLIES

G.P. Putnam's Sons New York

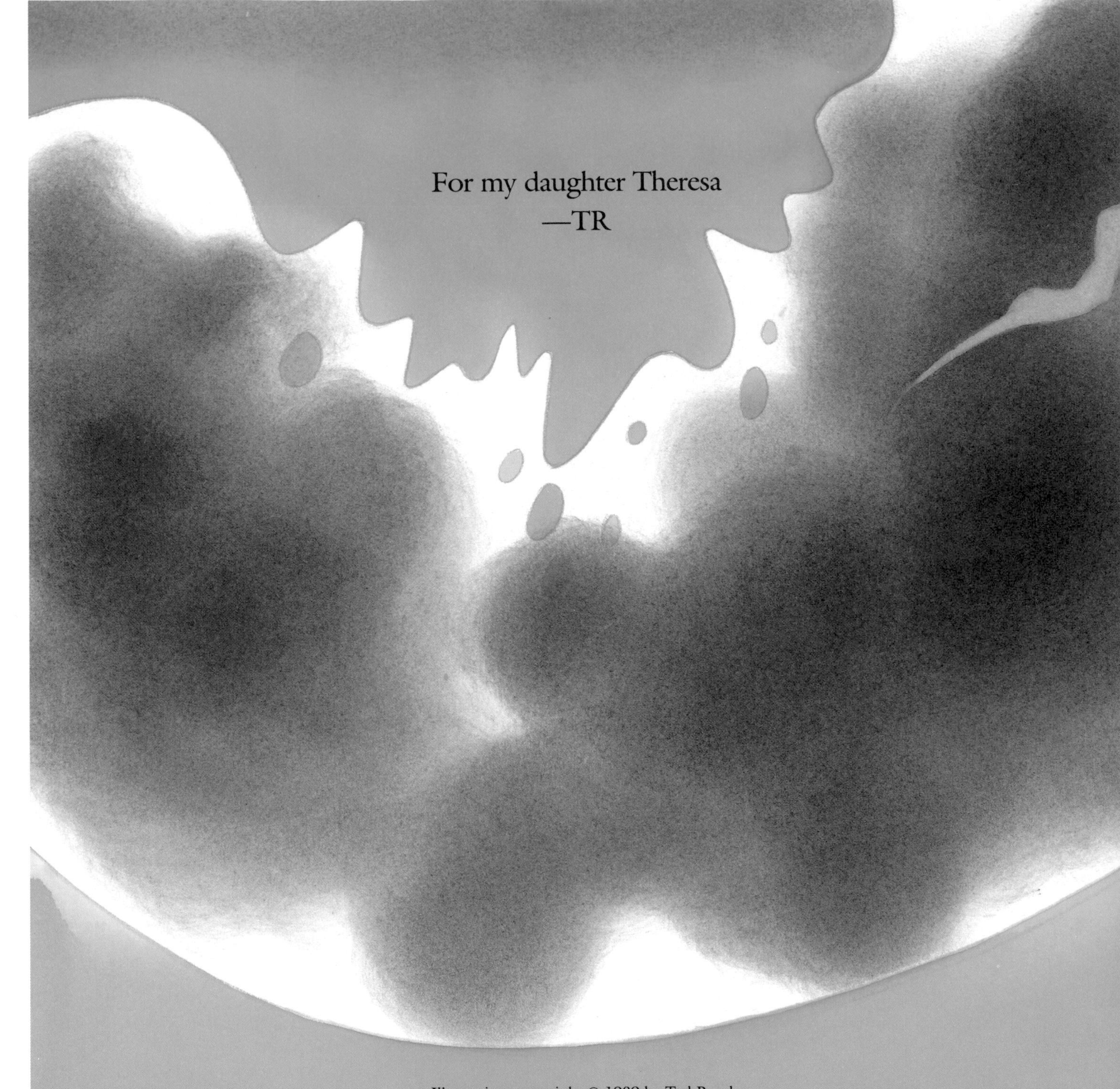

For my daughter Theresa
—TR

 Published simultaneously in Canada.
Printed in Hong Kong by South China Printing Co.
Typography by Golda Laurens

Library of Congress Cataloging-in-Publication Data
Lear, Edward, 1812-1888. The Jumblies / by Edward Lear ; illustrated by Ted Rand. p. cm.
Summary: The Jumblies go to sea in a sieve and have many adventures.
1. Children's poetry, English. [1. Nonsense verses. 2. English
poetry.] I. Rand. Ted, ill. II. Title.
PR4879.L2J8 1989 821'.8—dc19 88-11413 CIP AC
ISBN 0-399-21632-4

They went to sea in a sieve, they did;
In a sieve they went to sea:
In spite of all their friends could say,
On a winter's morn, on a stormy day,
In a sieve they went to sea.
And when the sieve turned round and round,
And every one cried, "You'll all be drowned!"
They called aloud, "Our sieve ain't big;
But we don't care a button, we don't care a fig:
In a sieve we'll go to sea!"
Far and few, far and few,
Are the lands where the Jumblies live:
Their heads are green, and their hands are blue;
And they went to sea in a sieve.

They sailed away in a sieve, they did,
In a sieve they sailed so fast,
With only a beautiful pea-green veil
Tied with a ribbon, by way of a sail,
To a small tobacco-pipe mast.
And every one said who saw them go,
"Oh! won't they be soon upset, you know?
For the sky is dark, and the voyage is long;
And, happen what may, it's extremely wrong
In a sieve to sail so fast."
Far and few, far and few,
Are the lands where the Jumblies live:
Their heads are green, and their hands are blue;
And they went to sea in a sieve.

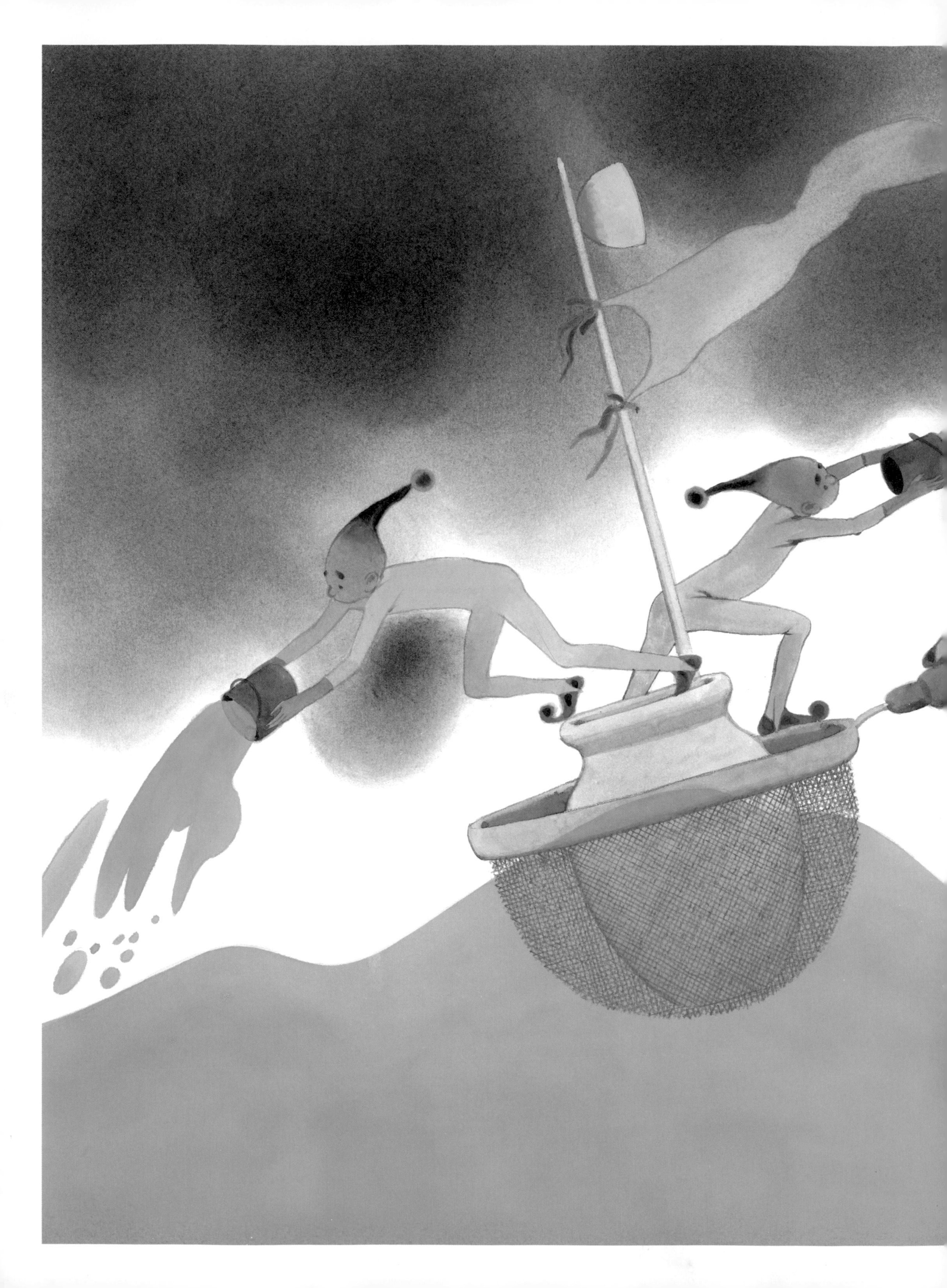

The water it soon came in, it did;
The water it soon came in:

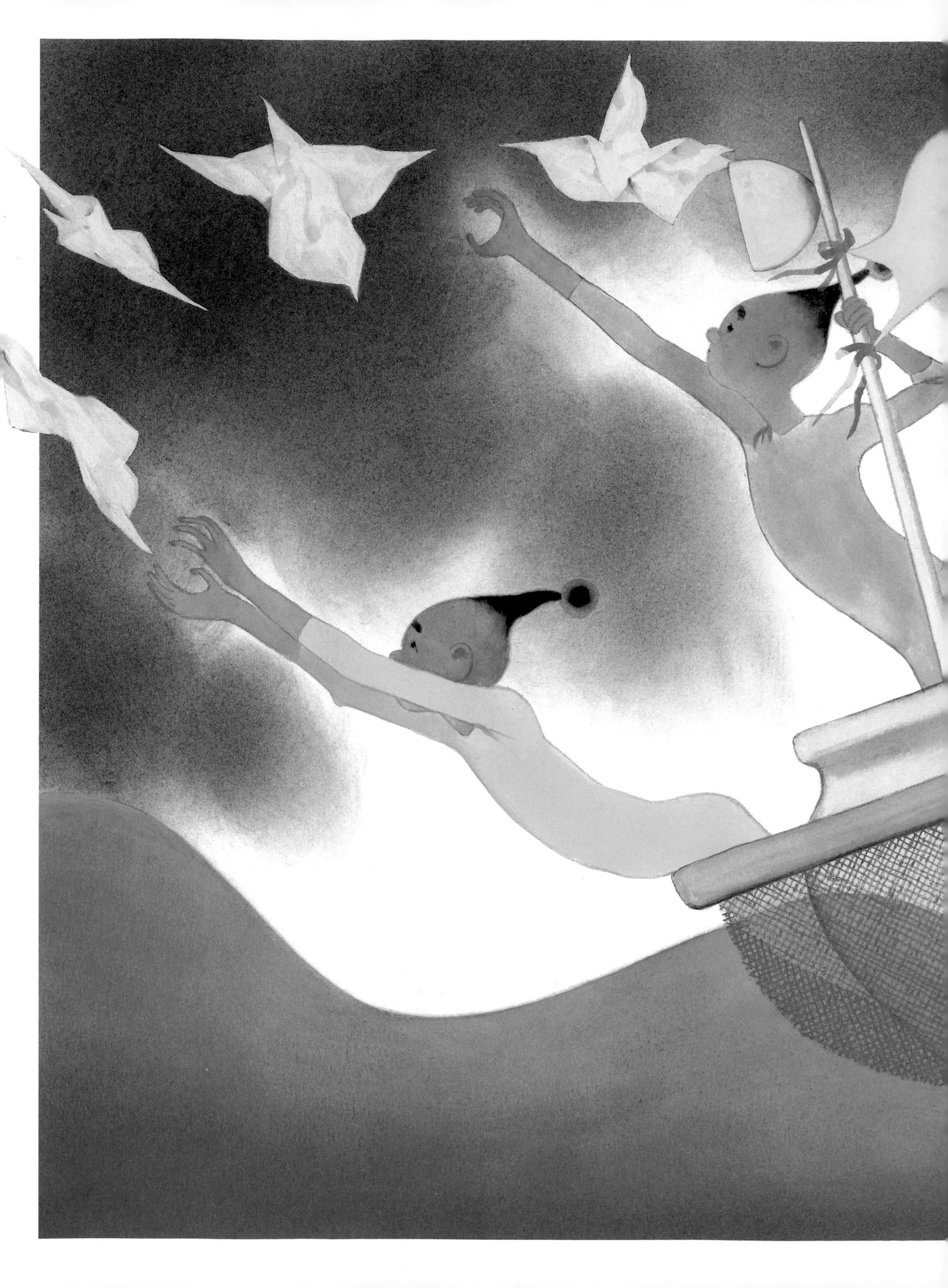

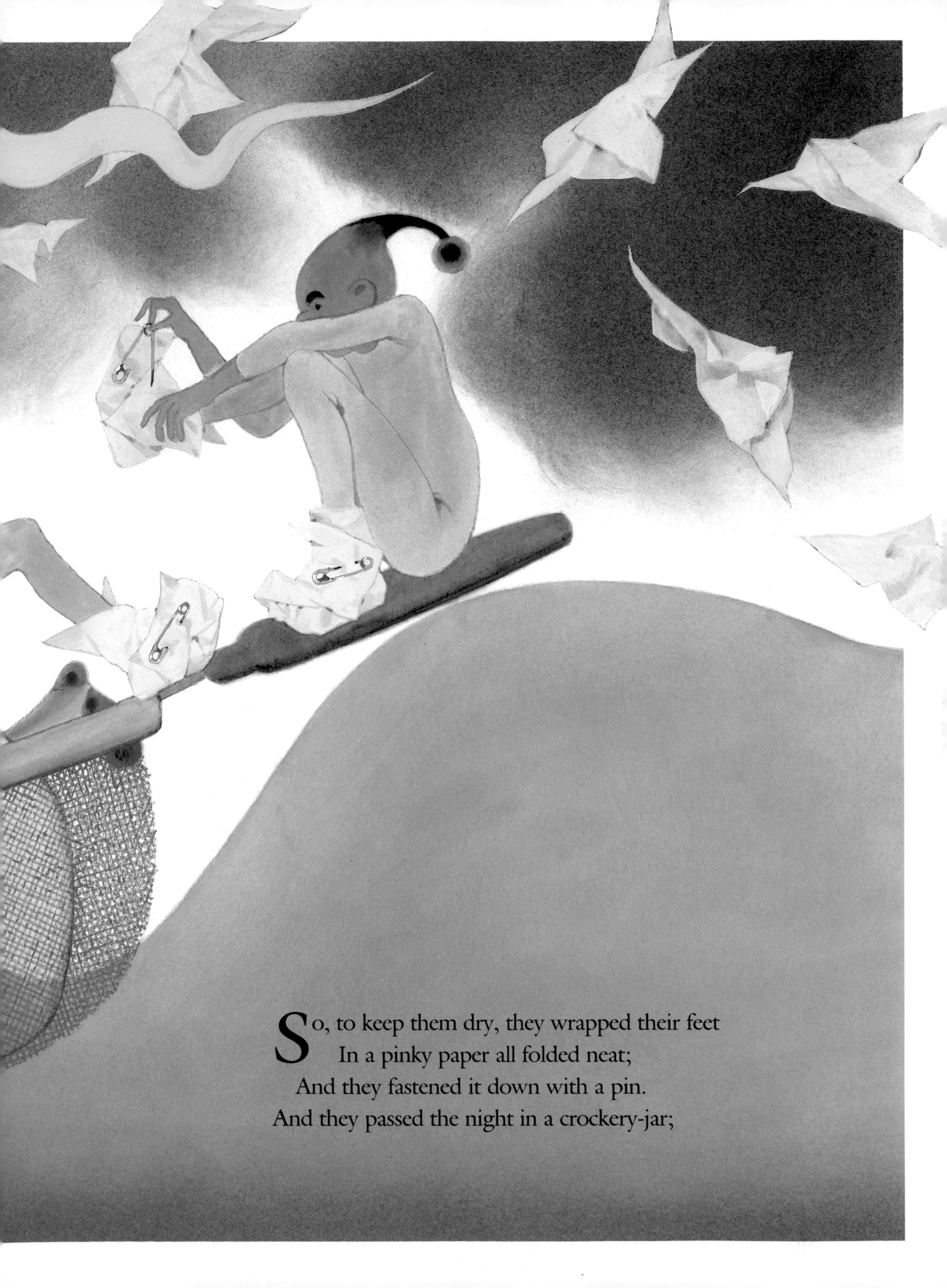

So, to keep them dry, they wrapped their feet
In a pinky paper all folded neat;
And they fastened it down with a pin.
And they passed the night in a crockery-jar;

And each of them said, "How wise we are!
Though the sky be dark, and the voyage be long,
Yet we never can think we were rash or wrong,
While round in our sieve we spin."
Far and few, far and few,
Are the lands where the Jumblies live:
Their heads are green, and their hands are blue;
And they went to sea in a sieve.

And all night long they sailed away;
And when the sun went down,
They whistled and warbled a moony song
To the echoing sound of a coppery gong,
In the shade of the mountains brown.
"O Timballoo! How happy we are
When we live in a sieve and a crockery-jar!
And all night long, in the moonlight pale,
We sail away with a pea-green sail
In the shade of the mountains brown."
Far and few, far and few,
Are the lands where the Jumblies live:
Their heads are green, and their hands are blue;
And they went to sea in a sieve.

They
sailed to
the Western Sea,
they did,—
To a land
all covered
with trees:

And they bought an owl,

And a useful cart,

And a pound of rice,

And a cranberry-tart,

And a hive of silvery bees;

And they bought a pig,

And some green jackdaws,

And a lovely monkey with lollipop paws,

And forty bottles of ring-bo-ree,

And no end of Stilton cheese.
Far and few, far and few,
Are the lands where the Jumblies live:
Their heads are green, and their hands are blue;
And they went to sea in a sieve.

And in twenty years they all came back,—
In twenty years or more;
And every one said, "How tall they've grown!
For they've been to the Lakes, and the Torrible Zone,
And the hills of the Chankly Bore."

And they drank their health, and gave them a feast
Of dumplings made of beautiful yeast;
And every one said, "If we only live,
We, too, will go to sea in a sieve,
To the hills of Chankly Bore."

Far and few, far and few,
Are the lands where the Jumblies live:
Their heads are green, and their hands are blue;
And they went to sea in a sieve.